A GIRL'S DREAM

SAI VARSHITHA CHIDIGE

ISBN 979-888530533-4

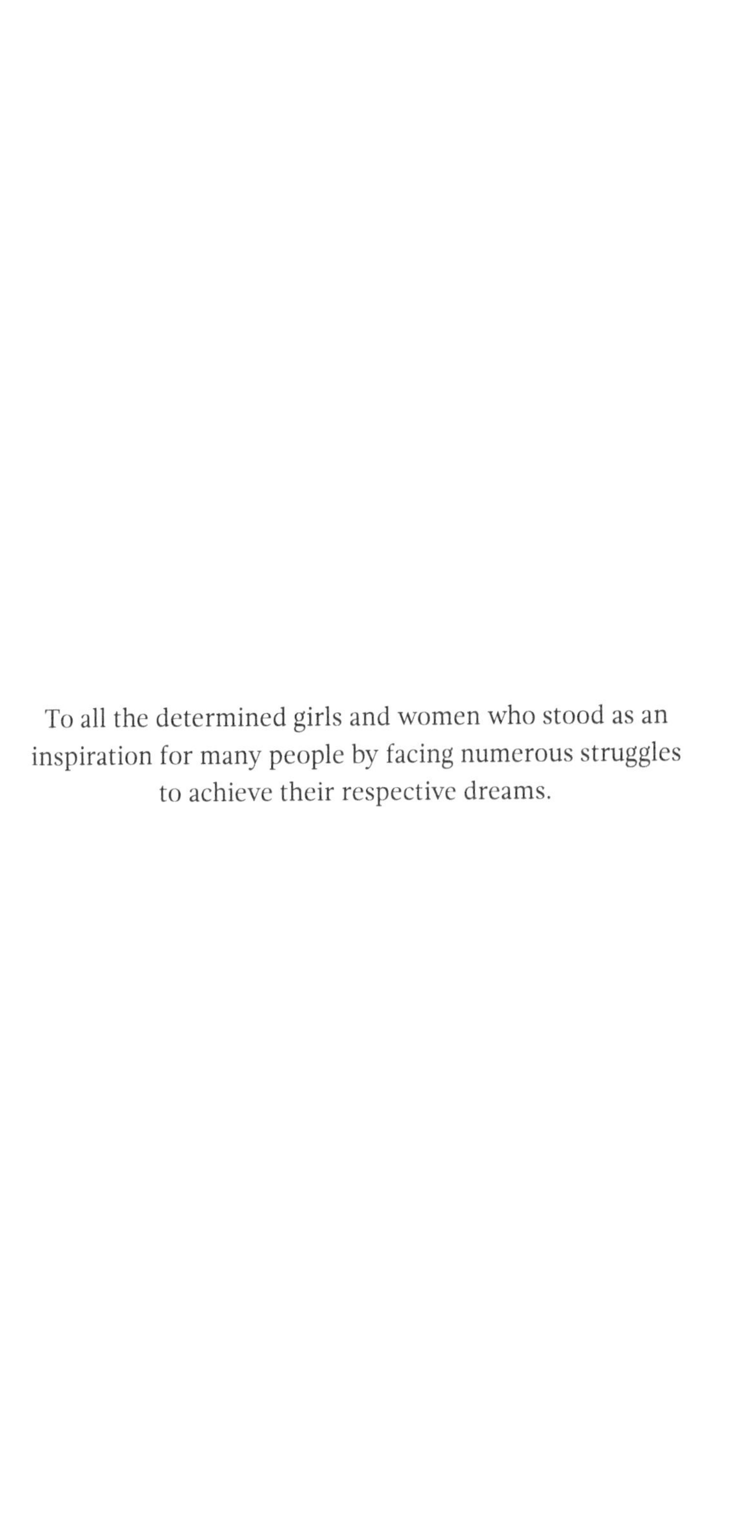

To all the determined girls and women who stood as an inspiration for many people by facing numerous struggles to achieve their respective dreams.

Contents

Contents

Epigraph

A dream is not something that you see while sleeping, it is something that does not let you sleep- APJ Abdul Kalam

Preface

This is my first ever novel. After exploring a few arts of entertainment, I thought of testing myself in Literary work. So, I eventually started writing five fictional stories at a time and after a few days, I found the story of a teenage girl is going great among all five and I started scouting more creatively for developing this story. And finally, I clustered all my thoughts together in developing this inspirational fictional story which includes mixed emotions of a teenage girl who cuts the Gordian knot to achieve her goal. After dodging many obstacles, she finally fulfills her dream with flying colors.

CHAPTER ONE

ME AND MY FAMILY

Shifting to the images section in Google, I said to myself by seeing an image of Miss Evana, an International model, "Oh! She looks great. What if I am her? I wish I were her".

By listening to the crackles of my room door, I put my mobile off and pretended to be reading my academic book. My mom came into my room, took a stick lying under the bed, and started beating me. She shouted by saying "An eighteen-year-old girl doesn't know how to handle a book in the correct position. Don't pretend as you are reading. You can't deceive your mother." Then I realized that I handled the book in the opposite direction hastily. My mother closed my room door and went away by giving an eccentric look. I am not very much upset as it is routine for me.

After a while, a couple of people came to my home and I excitedly looked out in search of new faces as I was bored of seeing my mother Maya and my moody mechanic father Raju. Listening to the people from the half-broken door of my room, I heard three words: some random date, bridegroom, and marriage. "Oh! Someone came to our home to invite us to a marriage," I said to myself. People went away after a sip of coffee.

I noticed a rare expression on my mom's face, i.e., her smile. Taking this as a chance, I went to my mom and asked for a new dress. She calmly went into the kitchen. I also went into my room by not uttering even a single word.

In the evening, my mom came to my room and exasperatedly said that she is leaving home for a few hours. I nodded my head and was elated inside. My mom locked the door and went away.

After taking a deep breath, I immediately took my mobile from the dusty shelf. I opened Google and searched for Miss Evana in the images section. I slipped into a new world by seeing her style, glam look, her way of talking, addressing, and whatnot. "She is the perfect example of a model," I said to myself.

Listening to the sound of anklets, I switched my mobile off, took books, and started reading hesitantly. I went near my room door when I heard a new voice. "Ah! It's my neighbor, Gayatri aunty," I said to myself. Aunty approached me and from the hollow of the door, she asked about my mother. "Aunty, mom is not at home. She went uh-hmm... somewhere" I told her. "That's Okay. How lucky are you? No one comes for my daughter," said aunty and left the place. I was baffled by her words. I left with no explanation for aunty's disappointment.

CHAPTER TWO

Time to Reveal me (The Narrator)

I went to the broken mirror in my room and stood in front of it where I could see my admirable and attractive eyes, a straight-edged nose, strawberry-colored lips, snow-colored skin tone, and coal-like long hair in different pieces of the mirror.

Posing in front of the mirror as a "MODEL", I expressed myself passionately by practicing the questions which were usually asked by Media to supermodels. I removed my dupatta, a permanent piece of clothing for me and started walking stylishly by leaving my hair down, which is waving just below my knees.

At around eight in the night, by hearing the sound of my father's motorbike, in a fraction of a second, I put on my dupatta, tied up my hair, and went out after making sure that everything was perfect. I saw my unpleasant mom next to my father.

My mother handed me the vegetable bag and asked me to follow her to prepare dinner. I gathered firewood and tried to blow air through a hollow pipe. My mother asked me to bring my academic notes. I panicked and brought notes from my room. She randomly picked one from a bunch of books and asked my Degree discontinued father to ask questions from it. My father grabbed the book from my sweaty hands, opened a page, and posed a question. I closed my eyes, comforted myself, remembered the question asked, and answered confidently as I am the concrete imbiber in a single session. My illiterate mother patted her eyes with happiness by listening to the answer told by me in English. Then, we all sat together for dinner to taste paratha with potato curry and replenish our stomachs.

The snoring of my father is disturbing me. I slept by pressing my pillow to my ears.

I got my Regular Dream...

"A very Young lady wearing a yellow gown is walking towards the crowd by leaving her hair down. She is stepping onto the stage fashionably by brushing her hair frequently with her hands. A bodyguard is following her to ensure security for her from the audience and fans. People are applauding by seeing her charming looks. Audience sounds and voices for her elegance are dominating her voice from speakers. Everyone is uttering her name with huge love towards her. She addresses the crowd by saying..."

"Hey, Wake up, it's already six in the morning," my mother yelled at me by showering a glass of water on my face. I woke up and searched for something new. But nothing changed. The same house, the same people, the same books, and the same me without freedom.

I completed my daily chores and when I was designing rangoli, Gayatri aunty came to my home and called my mother to prepare sweets at her house. My mom followed aunty and went away.

At around nine in the morning, my father also went to work by handing me all the responsibilities of the house.

I got ready to go to school as they called all the students for a small meeting in these Exam preparation holidays. I put on my uniform and started walking to my school, which is one kilometer away from my home. On the way, I kept on thinking about my family and my fate. "Many of my friends went to town to study. Their lifestyle is completely different from mine and they are happy souls. The main reason for my bad lifestyle is Modelling. My parents turned strict towards me from the time when the thought of modelling started in my mind. Usually, they are very kind, friendly, and affectionate parents," I said to myself.

After the meeting, I returned home alone. As it is the day of the weekly market in my village, my parents were not at home.

CHAPTER THREE

A Rude Decision

Suddenly, remembering Miss Evana's live show on YouTube, I took my mobile and continued observing her expressions, fluency, and dressing.

After the live show, I thought of practicing ramp walk. By moving my eyeballs around my room, I found a long threshold-like wooden material. I took it out and started practicing walking on it.

I raised my head astonishingly and immediately my eyes got covered with water. Instantly, my cheeks became red as cherries, my hands were as cold as the water in a mud pot because my mother was standing outside the room. She opened the door angrily, rebuked, hated me, and started crying for my behavior. I also started crying because of my mom's scolding.

"Are you my child? Don't you have concerns about your parents? How dare you think about modelling again, even after many conflicts, issues, and problems. Just two months ago, I requested you not to think about that useless career. The career you choose is useless because it won't suit our family, village, and lifestyle. I told you not to choose the field which is in contrast to our family. Boohoo! Now, I realised that you are not going to listen to my words anymore. So, I decided to stop you from being distracted by that field anymore. My decision is ….," said my mother by patting her wet eyes.

I was shocked when I heard her foolish decision. I screamed continuously for a long time and requested my mother to revert the decision. I pleased my mom to show some mercy on me.

"You are our one and only child Amisha. Every minute, me and your father think about you. You are our only world. We thought of making you study in any situation. But you went out of my control. Every mother strives for her child. In this situation, I suppose that my decision is the correct one. I am committed to my decision. This is over. Your stubborn and ignorant attitude made me take this decision," said my mother and went out.

I kept on wailing in my room and said to myself, "Marriage? How can she take such a rude decision? I am only 18 years old."

By continuously yowling, I recalled the moment when a couple of people came to my house, the day when I heard those three words: marriage, bridegroom, and some random date. "Huh! It's not someone's marriage. It's mine," I said to myself. Now I came to know the reason behind Gayathri aunty's praising words and her disappointment for her daughter.

I babbled and questioned myself by shedding tears, "Am I correct? Is my path wrong? Am I regretting my parents? Should a girl not relish choosing a path of her choice? Is marriage a complete solution to all of these issues? Am I a fool who achieved nothing in life?"

CHAPTER FOUR

MY PAST

In search of answers to all of these questions, I jogged my memory...

I was a fourteen-year-old girl, studying the ninth standard in a school in my village. I used to wake up at seven in the morning, complete my daily chores and get ready for school. My mom packs food for me and my father drops me at school on his motorbike. I was a very studious and focused girl.

Once, a newcomer of my class Catherine sat beside me, and within a few minutes, we became close to each other. She said to me, "How pretty you are. You have a very attractive face. You are the most glamorous girl in our entire village." I was delighted by her comments.

When I was twelve years old, many of my teachers, students, and villagers praised my beauty and compared my appearance with top actresses, but I just ignored their words as I have no interest in my looks at such a tender age. Some people even suggested I try my luck in movies. All these series of issues created a base for choosing a fashionable career.

At the age of seventeen years, some eminent personalities charmed the function in our village. I along with many of my classmates performed a drama by representing our school.

After the completion of the ceremony, a barrel-chested brawny man wearing a black shirt and black trousers approached me and asked me to follow him. I followed him with fear and hesitation.

My footsteps took me to an eminent actress who came there as a chief guest. I got excited after seeing her. The actress asked my name and said a great sentence that impacted me a lot i.e., "You are exactly looking like Miss Evana, a top model." I was elated to the next world for the words of an eminent actress. The Actress said, "Your face can impact a lot of the audience. You are a superstar among all-stars though you spread less light, what do I mean is, you played a very small role in a drama, but everyone got attracted to you. If you shine, that will create a huge positive impact on you. Shine yourself and show yourself to the world."

From her words, I came to know the importance of my face. "People got fascinated about me just for a very small role in a drama. What if I played the main role?" I said to myself. From that point in time, I started thinking about the modelling field.

After going home, I described the praising words of the actress to my parents happily. My mom just smiled at my eagerness and said, "You might have been tired. Go and sleep, Amisha." My parents ignored that incident.

After a few days, some people from the city came to our school and gave awareness about various activities and careers other than education. I took no notice of their words. By listening to word Modelling, I looked at them. They included modelling as one of the careers among Dancing, Singing, Instrument playing, Painting, Acting,

Monologue, and so on.

I excitedly went to them and requested to summarize the opportunities in the field of modelling. They were baffled at me because at such a young age, I asked them about the most glamorous and commercial sphere.

As it was their obligation to answer me, they briefed me about the first phase of the competition by ROW Co. Ltd. (Ramp on your way company limited), a leading company. I focused on their words, they gave a botox smile at me and left the place.

CHAPTER FIVE

My Mother's Concern

Hearing the door crackles, I came out of my memories. It's my mother who came to call me for dinner. I hesitantly followed her. Serving dinner to me and my father, my mom conveyed about various difficulties they faced for me. She said, "I and your father think only about your future and studies. Even though it is difficult for us to send you to the top school in our village, we are equally managing our responsibilities at home along with your studies. Your age is known as the 'Age of distraction.' As responsible parents, we want to give our best to our daughter. I don't have any hope of success in that voguish field. We hauled you to this position and we can't bear to consider anything wrong in the future. Also, the field opted by you is no way better than studying. Studies will never destroy or distract you. We have no guts to send you to that commercial and stylish path. Though your dad talks less, he is equally suffering from a huge pain in his heart for your bad choice. You are our loving angel Amisha. Please don't hurt us in this matter. Hope you mind my words. And there is good news for you, the groom has approved for continuation of your studies even after the marriage."

I zipped my mouth, had dinner, and went to sleep. I slept by remembering my mom's behavior and activities after knowing about my interest.

In the past, after hearing from officials who came to my school, I came to my mother very excitedly and explained about various careers including modelling. When I told my mom about that field, my mom noticed extreme happiness in me and she felt upset because of my distraction from studies.

As a villager, my mom doesn't know the literal meaning of this field. She filled her mind with a view that this field is uncomfortable, materialistic, negatively elegant, badly posing. The main concern for my mother is about my marriage. She was of the view that no one comes for me if I step into this glamorous platform.

Though it has many negative effects, she researched to know about modelling for my interest, happiness, and comfort. But, she couldn't digest herself to see me posing and dressing weirdly. She also tried to convince me by saying that it wouldn't be possible to succeed in this career without recommendations, money, and support.

Finally, my mother decided to restrict me only to studies. So, my mom became strict from then on.

CHAPTER SIX

I ROLLED UP MY SLEEVES FOR MY PASSION

Once, I was unable to control my interest and feelings towards modelling. So, I started concentrating on the first phase of the competition by ROW Co. Ltd., about which I came to know from the people who came to my village. Relying only on my knowledge, I completed the first phase secretly and posted my research work on the given project in the post once.

My Dream at night...

"Great directors were waiting for the appointment of a beautiful, gorgeous and elegant lady. Many Photographers lingered for her dates. All National Magazines were asking her for a cover photo in the magazine. Miss Evana, a well-known model, called her for dinner."

I woke up immediately, came out of my dream, and shook my head. By seeing the faces of my mother and father, I slapped myself by saying, "I am not eligible to become a model. It makes my family sad. I will stop thinking about my interests."

After a few days, my parents went to the city for my relatives' marriage. I took out my academic books and started studying with no interest. Hearing my name from outside, I went out. A postman came to our house and gave me a post, which was in my name.

I got confused and opened the post. My happy tears rolled down after reading the letter. I took that post close to my heart and said to myself, "Thank you ROW Co. Ltd."

It's the acceptance and qualifying letter from ROW Co. Ltd. And they also sent a small box in which there was a mobile. I was overwhelmed by that unexpected situation. In those types of situations, I felt that feelings are the greater source to express happiness.

The text on the letter reads as,

"Congratulations Amisha. We are delighted to inform you that you have been selected for Phase 2 of the Project Competition. We are hoping to see you on the final list of this project. Best of luck."

After taking a look at the given statistics, "Oh my God! I am one among the eighteen ladies," I said to myself. From then, hope arose in me to step into this field, and then I decided not to turn back from this competition.

THERE ENDS MY PAST

CHAPTER SEVEN

THE PRESENT

In the present day morning, while sweeping my home, I found a bundle of papers under the rice bag. I took the papers out and felt very happy by seeing those research papers of the Phase 2 competition. I folded them and secretly kept them in my dupatta.

I sat in my room to finalize the project of ROW Co. Ltd as there are only a few days left for submission. But, after remembering the words and rude decision of my mom a few months back, I kept the papers aside and took my books as an obligation.

On the spur of the moment, my friend Catherine came to my home and asked me about my preparation for exams during these holidays. I said, "I am preparing for my marriage, Catherine." Catherine was shocked and asked, "What about your modelling contest." After listening to the series of incidents that happened last night, she felt very sad, comforted me.

Going back to her home, she said, "Believe in yourself Amisha, the world will be at your feet." I got inspired by this quote which was said by Swami Vivekananda. I also remembered the quotation, "If you want to live a happy life, tie it to a goal, not to people or things" which was said by my teacher when talking about Einstein.

These two quotes made me mentally strong for proceeding further. I decided to set my sights on my goal. "My parents who are worrying now will feel happy about my success. As an orthodox mother, she made the correct decision for me as she doesn't want me to go into illusion. But, I am sorry mom. I want to go to the field of my interest and I am sure that you will feel proud of me in the future," I said to myself. I took a deep breath and marked in my mind to not change my mind at times my mom rebukes or convinces me.

I took my grimy phone back and searched for the submission date of the phase 2 project. I became upset as there are only two days left for posting my work in the office. "Oh, God! At least, I am left with no outline of the project for proceeding further," I said to myself. I consoled myself and set to tackle these circumstances for achieving my goal.

After a few hours, I came out of my room and found my parents repairing a table fan for my room. I lent them a hand and helped in fixing it.

By seeing me in a cheerful mood, my mother started observing my activities. We all had our dinner and my mom continuously focussed on me with a contrasting look. As she saw me in a different mood, my mother had multiple negative and positive thoughts at once on a smaller scale of time.

The next day, I completed all my daily activities quickly and decided to finish phase 2. As my parents are of the view that I am preparing for exams, no one disturbed me, so I proceeded with my work quite peacefully.

The Next day, I went to the post office, "Uncle, Please make sure that this post reaches the "To" address tomorrow," I said to the Postman. Contentedly and hastily, I started rushing back to my home because I said to my parents that I am leaving out to consult my teacher regarding a doubt in my studies.

But all of a sudden, I stopped by seeing a marriage ceremony between a very young girl and a person aged 30 years. Tears from my eyes didn't stop flowing as if the water from the open tap. "Marriage at a young age for a disinterested girl is a bane to her. How can their parents take such an impertinent decision? This is not at all fair. How savage are the people?" I said to myself.

I couldn't stop crying and immediately ran away from that place. I did no justice to the girl as I have no right to talk against that because, after a few months, I am also going to face the same.

I returned home and my mind completely got filled with the derogatory word 'marriage.'

CHAPTER EIGHT

THE DAY WHEN I MET 'HIM'

In the Evening, after filtering my mind by removing unnecessary thoughts, I went upstairs to hang the washed clothes. Then I saw him.

A teenage boy with bristly eyebrows, a hawkish nose, Titan's shoulders, and leopard-like grace is standing in front of my house. I saw him and immediately turned my head as I was pretending to ignore him. He continuously stared at me for 5-7 minutes. After a few minutes, he called me by saying "Hey! Excuse me. Please come down."

I stood on my terrace with fear because a meeting between a strange boy and a girl is something weird in villages. By listening to him, my mom came out with a rude face and asked him the reason for calling. He managed by saying, "Hello Aunty, I am from XYZ bank and I am here to say that you have won a lottery ticket worth ten thousand rupees." My mom became overwhelmed by listening to him and welcomed the boy to our balcony.

In the meantime, I went into my room. My mom asked him to explain the lottery details. Then he intelligently deceived my mom by saying, "Aunty, only a literate person of the family can understand my explanation." My mom called me and made me sit in front of him. I understood that the boy was trying to flirt with me. But my mother is unable to understand his intention.

I restively sat by managing myself to not get trapped into his blazing eyes. He continuously spoke some random stuff about that fake lottery ticket in front of my mom. My mother went into the kitchen to bring coffee. Giving a striking look at me, he said, "Hello! Miss Amisha, a beauty ambassador." The word that locked both of our eyes is 'Miss'. I raised my head and saw him because I am in love with that word as I want to officially see my name with the word 'Miss' in the fashionable world.

He said, "You know? I have been following you for the past two years. I don't want to lag my feelings towards you anymore. I like you uh-huh-hmm...I love you. I am saying this with a huge responsibility; I will be with you in hard times. Will you follow in my footsteps?"

I bashfully went into my room. My cheeks got red as cherries, my lips were smiling for no reason and my hands became very cool.

Then, my mom called me to serve him coffee as she was busy talking with my father on the phone. I approached him and offered him a drink. While turning back, he called me and said, "Reply to me." By listening to my mom's anklets' sound, he left my hand and said, "I am hoping for a positive response." After a sip of coffee, he left the place by placing a packed cover in my hand and gesturing to me "goodbye".

Various thoughts started running in my mind at once. I was surprised after opening his cover. "God!!! I am Damn' happy. I got exhausted by searching for this. This is my favorite book ever. How did he find this? In between, how did he come to know my interest in this book? My mom always says that the only nearest and dearest ones understand our feelings. But, it was the first time I met him. Within this glimpse of time, I feel that there is a strong bond between us. Ahh! It's a different feeling. Is he my childhood friend? Is he my relative? Bah! It's a waste of time to think about him. I am slowly getting distracted. This should not happen. But, his words and looks are luring me. Okay well, what's done is done. Ugh! I don't want to divert from my goal. I will just thank him tomorrow for giving me this expensive modelling book. I will cut my side with the word 'thanks.' So that he won't keep any expectations on me," I said to myself and slept after having dinner.

The very next day, expecting the young boy's presence for me, I woke up early in the morning, completed my daily chores quickly, and stood at my room door waiting for him. My mom and dad went to the president of our village to request some money for interest.

Just then, listening to the shoe sound, I quickly went into my room, patted my face with some talcum powder, and wore my dupatta only on one of my shoulders, which is the ongoing trend in my village for young girls. By bending my head, I went to him and said, "I don't know your intention on me but I just want to confirm that-uh-err....." I slowly raised my head and saw a gentleman with a teachable posture and great gratitude. I said "Hey, who uh-ah-err- you. Ahh-uh-if you have any work with my father, come after some time. He went out for some work."

"Hello Amisha, I am Jatin," he said.

"So what? In fact, how do you know my name? Are you following me? See, I don't want to make this an issue...," his voice stopped me.

"Excuse me. I am Jatin, your fiancé," he said politely.

"So, What if you are my fia-aa-n-uh-err- I'm sorry" I hesitantly apologized to him.

"It's Okay. Hope you are doing well. This is our first meeting, right? By the way, you look beautiful. I brought you something. Guess what?" he questioned me.

I am very bashful at him and I at least didn't offer him some water. With tense, I continued behaving rudely and I am also left with no conversation to talk with him. I answered all his questions by giving a fake smile at him.

"Anyway, Nice to meet you. Take this box as my pre-wedding gift," he said and went back in a hatchback white-colored car.

"I don't know what happened in the last few minutes. Why didn't I tell him about my goal and request to cancel the marriage? I behaved abnormally", I said to myself and opened the gift given by him.

"Mad! How can he expect me to wear this dress? It's not even a dress; it's just a one-piece black knee-length dress. Doesn't he have any common sense? How can a village girl accept this?," I got frustrated.

CHAPTER NINE

THOSE STRESSFUL DAYS

After two days, the day is the most stressful in my life because the results of the phase 2 competition will be out. Pushing the door, my mom came to my room and said, "Hey, your engagement date got fixed. Groom wants his marriage to be completed very soon as he likes you. So, no more ways for you other than nodding your head for my words. Engagement is going to be held in the city. Be proud of being the wife of a knowledgeable, stylish and handsome man."

I listened to my mother's words ignorantly and went to the balcony to get a chance to go to the post office. But my mother is busy cleaning the house and it seems that she won't step outside today.

Then the young boy came to my home with a letter in his hand. He quietly placed a letter in my hand and went away.

"Hmm...I guess it's a love letter. What else I can expect from him other than this," I said to myself and opened the cover of the letter.

"Oh my God! My dream is not so far away. I couldn't believe my selection for phase 3 of the competition. Oh! It seems the boy went to the post office and brought this letter for me. I misunderstood him. He intends to help me in every problem," I formed a good opinion of the young boy.

The Letter reads as,

"From ROW Co. Ltd. (Ramp on your way company limited). Dear Amisha, Congratulations. You have got selected for the last phase of the competition. And it is delightful to inform you that you are one of the top 50 candidates who are the finalists of this competition. We are hoping to see you on the final list. Please fill the form and send it. Regards, ROW Co. Ltd."

This letter boosted my confidence a lot and it's time to fill out the form and send it.

"Oh gosh! Authority is asking for my account name on all social media platforms. Girls like me are not even allowed to use mobiles, how can they expect a social media account. But I have to move forward by catching up with the developing world. The time has come for me to create an account. But I don't know the process to do it. The only option left for me is to ask for help and the right person for this is the young boy," I said to myself.

In the evening, the boy stood under a tree in front of my home. I gestured to him to say his mobile number. He was surprised and by showing his fingers, he gestured to me his number. I immediately went into my room and dialed him.

"Amisha, how lucky I am. The future top model dialed me. How can I believe this?" he said on the phone.

"Don't act too smart. I just called you for help. Don't keep any expectations on me. If you are ready to help me, I will proceed further, otherwise, I am gonna block your number on my mobile," I talked to him rudely as it is a powerful weapon for any teenage girl against boys.

"Hey girl, I am here to help you. I will do anything for you. What's the matter," he asked.

I briefed the whole problem about the account. He asked me to chill and after a few minutes, he created an account in my name and messaged me the details of it.

As there are only two days left for the submission of phase 3 work, I completed all my work quickly and posted it in the post office with the help of a young boy.

After two days, the time has come for the results of phase 3 of the competition.

To ease my stress, I took my mobile and saw 103 people who have sent me friend requests. Seeing all, I figured out one familiar face. "Oh! The name of the young boy is Neel. I think he is very good at photography, his pictures are amazing," I said to myself.

The next minute, I received a direct message. The message reads as,

"Hey Amisha, We are glad to inform you that you got shortlisted for a saree photoshoot. We liked your work for phase 1 and phase 2 of the Competition conducted by ROW Co. Ltd. Grab the opportunity and text a message to the number 946*****54. Regards, Fashion in saree Co. Ltd. (FIS)"

I noticed many messages from various well-known companies and well-known modelling hubs, which texted me for interviews, photoshoots, and advertisement shootings. I got shocked at these hundreds of messages. I just ignored all the messages because my main goal is to hit the arrow on the big competition of ROW Co. Ltd.

CHAPTER TEN

SCREAMED, SHOUTED AND STOPPED

Listening to the sound of Neel, I went out and asked him about the result. He cringed his head and nodded horizontally. I stood in front of him by shedding my silent tears. He grabbed my hand to console me. I pulled back my hand and ran into my room.

Screaming in my room, I said "my dream has an expiry date, I need to accomplish it before it gets expired i.e., before my marriage. But now, I am left with no option but just to nod my head for my mom's decision. Now, I just have to marry a stranger and be stuck in his home as an anonymous person to the world. I thought of managing my parents by succeeding in this competition, but my hard work just went like a dead horse."

The next day,

"Huh! How it would be if I were in the place of this competition winner. The winner's parents were interviewed by many news channels and the fashion magazines displayed her image with the title 'The young intellectual model.' She was also awarded a cash prize worth one lakh rupees. Moreover, the memento was handed over by Miss Evana, who is my favorite. What else is required for an eighteen-year-old girl?" I murmured to myself.

After a few minutes, my phone beeped for a message. The message reads as,

"We are glad to inform you that you got selected to avail a free modelling course from one of the leading companies in India WYR Co. Ltd. (The world is your runway company limited). As we loved your presence of writing, the logical texture, and the overall work in the competition of the ROW Co. Ltd., we are offering you this amazing opportunity to learn and get great experience with the most eminent models. You are among the twenty people who were chosen to learn with us. For any further queries please contact 927*****78."

"Modelling course? Is this true? WYR Co. Ltd. is such a big company," I said to myself and regained hope. I texted all my queries about the place and duration.

After two days, Neel sent me a message,

"Hello! Girl, hope you are well. This is the first time I haven't seen you continuously for two days. I am away from you to give you some space for getting out of the trauma. If there is an availability of all the reliable and advanced sources, for a determined girl like you, it is easy to be on the final list. Don't step back from your career for only one minor failure. Be strong and grab all the flowers like opportunities to wear the garland of success around your neck. Hope we meet soon. All the best my dear."

I wore a little smile on my face with the message and I immediately swiped my phone to read the answers sent by WYR Co. Ltd for my queries.

"Ah! It's going to be held in Maraasi city and that too for a month. How can I manage it? Oh no, they also asked me to send a few pictures of mine in western wear. I am from an orthodox family where girls are not even allowed to go out without a dupatta. I am sure that I am not going to do this," I said to myself by shutting my mobile off to sleep.

CHAPTER ELEVEN

TICKET OR FIANCÉ

The next morning, I noticed my mom and dad feeling tense. My mom is wandering from one corner of the house to the other corner by knotting flowers. She asked me to wear a half-saree. My mother is not even answering my question about this rush. I went into my room and got ready. Hearing the welcoming wishes, I looked out from my room and saw my In-laws and fiancé.

I offered them some sweets and coffee as my mother forced me to do that. My father, in-laws, and bridegroom sat on chairs and I was made to sit down by my mother-in-law. Groom asked my father's permission to talk with me. My father hesitantly approved and we both went to the balcony.

"Hey Amisha, how are you? You are looking more beautiful today. I know that you are feeling inconvenient to face me, umm-but I have one wish which you can fulfill. That is...ah-uh-err-can you please wear the dress which I gave you," he asked.

I am happy to wear it. Because no one will object to me if I wear it now at the request of Jatin. Also, I got a chance to click some photos for sending them to the WYR Co. Ltd.

I accepted his request and went into my room. I wore the dress and saw myself in the mirror. I noticed it as a strange and different look. The one in the mirror looked like my twin, who was brought up in the city. As there is little time for me, with the long braid and messy face, I clicked a photo myself, sent it quickly to the WYR Co. Ltd., and then went out. My mom and dad gave a strange look at me and my mom said, "Are you mad? Why did you wear this dress? Who offered this dress to you? Who is that stupid? "

"Mom, the stupid is the groom," I replied

"Ehhh-err-it's okay. No problem, you can wear it. This is the right age for you to wear these types of dresses," my mom managed in front of in-laws.

I went to Jatin bashfully. "Wow! Awesome, you are looking gorgeous in every look. Thank you for wearing this for me," he said and after some time, they left the place.

"Only three days were left for joining in the free modelling contest. I have to take someone's help to get an idea. Yes! Neel is the correct person to ask for. Let me text him," I said to myself.

I texted Neel about the fixation of my engagement date and also about the offer from WYR Co. Ltd. Within a few minutes, I got a message from him, which read, "Come out." I rushed out. He handed over a train ticket to me and said, "I also bought the ticket and I will be waiting for you at the station the day after tomorrow." After saying this, he immediately left the place as my parents were at home.

I placed the photo of my fiancé on one side and the train ticket to Maraasi city on the other side. "Life with my fancé will not give me any special identity. I will be the person stuck around the four walls of the house. Whereas life with my favorite career will be the best. Modelling is my passion, my love, my goal, my self-respect, and everything," I said to myself and took the train ticket to my heart.

"But how can I believe Neel? My heart believes him as a well-wisher, but my mind is signaling not to believe him. But, as Neel is the only option left for me, I have to adjust and go with him. Alas! Though I wish to go with him, it's not easy to manage my parents. I don't want to keep any expectations of going to the city. Please help me god," I said to myself.

The next day, my mother called me and said, "Amisha, I want to talk about an important thing with you. Groom is interested in shopping with you for engagement. His mother went abroad to look after her daughter, who is bearing a child now. Her father is busy with some important contract, which is not letting him stay with the groom. So if you don't mind, uh-err can you please go to the city and help him in shopping and look after things."

"Am I his wife? How can he ask me to shop with him, that too without his parents? This clearly shows his bad manners. Mom, at least you might have thought about this right? Mom, I am sorry. I am not going anywhere," I shouted and went to sleep.

The very next day, I sat on the balcony sadly as that is the day on which we have to go to the company in the city.

My father interrupted my thoughts, sat beside me, and said, "Dear daughter, I didn't ask for any favor from you till now. But it's time for me to ask. Jatin is a very good and well-mannered boy. Believe him with faith. In a few months, he will be your husband, who will provide the best for you for the rest of your life. If he can bear you for years, can't you bear him just for two months? I can understand that any girl fears living with a stranger. But believe me,

Jatin is a very good boy. He arranged a separate room for you in the hotel. I am sure that you will feel safe and secure with him. Hope you listen to this father's words. Will you?" asked my father.

As it is for the first time, my father talked to me emotionally and with the utmost request, I couldn't ignore his words, So, I approved to go to the city.

CHAPTER TWELVE

A Village Girl in the City

Immediately my mother packed my things and said, "Be safe my girl. For the first time, we are leaving you alone." My father gave me the ticket and greeted me.

In the railway station, I saw Neel and asked, "Hey, why are you here?"

"The train will arrive in twenty minutes. Be ready," he replied.

I explained to him the entire incident. He felt very sad and consoled me for missing a good chance of training with the eminent models.

"Anyway, I will be here till the train arrives," he said

The train arrived and I walked towards my compartment, then Neel's voice stopped me.

"Amisha, is this the correct train?" he asked.

"Yes, the train number on my ticket and the train is the same," I replied.

He came close to me, grabbed the ticket from my hands, shouted with happiness, and said, "This is the Balghed express which takes us to Maraasi."

"No, Maraasi is the place where WYR Co. Ltd. is located. Now I want to go to the city in which my fiancé is living," I replied.

"Mad! The city in which your fiancé is staying is the Maraasi city," he said.

"Oh! Really! I am damn happy," I expressed my extreme happiness.

"Quick, the train is about to leave. Come on, step in," he shouted.

We both went into the compartment and took a deep breath. I thanked God immensely for clearing the obstructed debris on my path to achieve the goal.

"But there is a problem with my fiancé. I have to manage him with utmost care. He is a very intelligent man," I said to Neel.

"Don't worry. You can. If he is intelligent, you are the most intelligent girl. Your determination towards your goal will make you do anything," he inspired me.

"Well, what about some shopping after we get down from the train?" he asked.

"Shopping? Why is it necessary? I brought my clothes from home," I said.

"All of your clothes will be churidars. But as you are stepping into the glamorous field, you should buy a few clothes that suit the sphere in which you are entering," he said.

But,... (I interrupted him)

"Don't say anything, just listen to me. I had grown up in the city. I am completely aware of the lifestyle here. I will change your look completely. If you want to see yourself equally with your co-students in the WYR Co. Ltd., listen to me," he said.

I just nodded my head as it is for the first time I am entering the city. Moreover, I know nothing about the city's culture. Also, I want to see myself highlighted among all people in the office.

CHAPTER THIRTEEN

CHURIDAAR TO JEANS; BRAID TO BANGS

We stepped down from the train and moved towards a six-floored shopping mall. I looked at everyone weirdly as no one was wearing a churidar. "Huh! Awkward, how can these ladies wear a waist-length T-shirt and tightened trousers. Did they feel comfortable in these types of dresses?" I questioned Neel.

"Yes, once you observe them, they are giving you a weird look as you are wearing a traditional dress and a long braid. Let's go to a parlor after shopping," he said.

"Parlour? I am not hungry. What is the need of going to an Icecream Parlour now?" I said.

"Haha, I am talking about a Beauty parlor. Let's go there to change your hairstyle," Neel said.

"Why? I love my hair. I don't want any unnecessary machines to rub on my head. It will damage my hair," I resisted.

"Once imagine yourself in a western look with a long braid. How dirty it looks. Listen to me. You will like your look after your haircut," he tried to convince me.

"Okay, but there is not enough money with me," I said.

"Don't worry. I will bear the burden of charges. You just nod your head for my words," he said.

I agreed with him and we started our shopping. I stood aside from the clothes displayed as I didn't like at least one dress. Many trousers which were torn, waists lengthen tops and other dresses were hung.

Neel took out a red tank top with black stripes and denim blue jeans. I thought that he took these clothes for someone in their family. But he came to me and said, "Try these clothes."

I was shocked and ignored wearing it. But he insisted and convinced me to try the dress.

"I hesitantly wore and came out of the trial room. "Oh my goodness, this look perfectly suits your white skin tone. I am very much satisfied with the dress. Let's buy it," he expressed his excitement.

After buying some more clothes, we went to the billing session. "Huh! The total bill is 22,000 rupees for buying only six sets of clothes?" I questioned Neel.

"Yes, lifestyle in the city is expensive," replied Neel.

We moved to a beauty parlor for my haircut. The people in the parlor confused me by saying many names of haircuts. Neel replied to their questions and asked them to cut bangs.

After a while, I thanked Neel for recommending such a beautiful style to me.

"As we will be heading to the WYR Co. Ltd now, it's better to wear one of the dresses we bought from the shop," Neel said.

"But how can I manage my fiancé with this look?" I asked Neel.

"It's better to face Jatin in a stylish look because he won't question you in further days even if he sees you somewhere outside the city. Manage him by saying that you wore this trendy dress for him. He likes the western wear right?" Neel questioned me.

"Yes, Earlier when he came to our village, he gave me a modish dress and insisted I wear it for him," I replied.

"Then fine. There will be no problem with Jatin. As of now, go into a room and change your dress in the parlor itself. Let's move to the office," Neel said.

I came out wearing a bell-handed white shirt with boot-cut black jeans. The staff in the parlor were shocked after seeing my look. "Ma'am, your look and style got completely changed. Can I give you a suggestion? Leave your hair down for a more elegant look," said a lady in the parlor.

As everyone is giving an awed look at me, I felt shy at first but after listening to their praising comments, I felt very proud of myself and we started our journey to the WYR Co. Ltd. on a metro train.

CHAPTER FOURTEEN

AT WORK

Neel said that he will be waiting outside for me. I stepped into one of the huge buildings in Maraasi city. Straight away, I went to the office's reception to enquire about the admission process. The receptionist called someone and sent her with me.

"Hello, ma'am. I am Urvi. You are the last one to join this course. Your co-students have completed their process already. Ma'am, let me show you the modelling hall where you will be trained from tomorrow," said the lady with me.

"Okay, Urvi. In between, who is that voguish lady with a classy walk" I asked Urvi by pointing my finger towards a posh lady.

"Ma'am, her name is Fara. She is one of the most notable models in India. Do you know? She was one of the finalists along with Miss Evana in the 'Mela Fiesta fashion show'. She will be your trainer for one month" Urvi replied.

I said "Oh!! I am very excited as the model who worked with Miss Evana is going to train me." With the same zeal, I stepped into the Modelling hall where my happiness dwindled. There were around twenty big posters of all the applicants. Posters were hung down from the third floor of the building to the ground floor. Everyone's look in the posters is dashing, their posture, hairstyle, and everything are debonair. But the poster of me among all the others is odd. My photo on the poster is the click that was sent by me to WYR Co. Ltd. on the day when Jatin insisted I wear the dress given by him. Compared to all the posters, my look at the poster is horrible.

"Ma'am, is that you? I can't believe it. Now you are looking beautiful and chic. But in the poster, you are looking like a village girl," Urvi said.

"What do you know about a girl from the village? Village girls are hardcore among all people. Don't ever underestimate girls from villages. Mind your words," I rebuked the words of Urvi.

She apologized to me and took me to the Coordinator of this initiative. He is a soft-spoken person with a big heart. He congratulated me and wished for my success.

After completing all the formalities and application procedures, I and Neel went to the Railway Station. He dropped me there and went away to a hotel in the city.

CHAPTER FIFTEEN

MY FIANCÉ

I dialed Jatin and asked him to pick me up from the station. He came to the station in a grey business suit with a seven-fold tie and brown shoes. As he saw me in a half-saree and a long braid in the village, he didn't recognize me. So, I went to him and said, "Hello Jatin. I am Amisha."

He gave a contrasting look at me and said "Hey, I can notice a huge difference in you and your style. What's the matter? Is anything special?" he questioned.

"Hee-hee, the whole change in my look is only for you Mr. Jatin. As you are fond of sophisticated looks, I stood before you in this way," I managed him.

We both reached one of the big hotels in the city.

"Did you like the hotel, Amisha? This is where I have been staying for the past three months. The quarters given by my company are undergoing renovation, so I shifted to this hotel," Jatin said.

"The hotel is too cozy and reflects its elegance. But how are you managing the huge charges by the hotel?" I questioned Jatin.

"As my salary is more than enough for me, I am in no way concerned about the expenses here. My parents are well settled who don't expect a rupee from me. As a young gentleman, I too have no big plans of investing money for the future," he replied.

"Hmm, my parents trawled the Rich man," I said to myself.

"Why did you like me? I mean, you are in a great position, there might be many girls waiting for you. But why did you select me?" I asked Jatin.

"Amisha, you are not an obligation for me. I didn't select you. 'Select' is the wrong word you choose. You are the only girl who made me feel that life will be incredibly happy with you. I was born in a village but I was completely brought up in the hostels of this city for my Education. Though I worked with many ladies, I never got the same feeling with anyone before. Do you know? Destiny put us together," Jatin said.

I listened to Jatin's words reluctantly and questioned, "Destiny? How can you say that?"

"When the mediator for marriage came to our house, he showed us the pictures of many girls. I just took a look at all the pictures and accepted none. Then, he scrolled your picture, which made me feel happy and fulfilled. When I asked the mediator about your details, he said that the photo got mixed up mistakenly and it's not possible to marry you. When I questioned him, he said about your poor condition and blah-blah-blah. I called my parents and asked to fix the marriage with you. As my parents got fed up with my criticizing words for marriage, they felt happy and accepted you as their daughter-in-law. Huh! this is the story behind my proposal to marry you," said Jatin.

I just nodded my head and controlled myself to not let me go towards his side and marry him without fulfilling my dream. After some time, I and Jatin went to a shopping mall to shop for a few clothes for marriage and casual days.

In the Shopping mall, "Hey Amisha, will you try this for me," he asked me by showing a half-shoulder clingy blue-colored top and a Flared cocktail pink-cloured skirt.

He thought that I will ignore trying this. He is still of the opinion that I am a village girl, who always wears conservative clothes. As I completely got fond of this trendy wear, I accepted it to try it.

After our dinner, we returned to the hotel with seven bags of clothes. He dropped me in my room and went to his room.

CHAPTER SIXTEEN

I TORE HIM OFF A STRIP

After three days, once in the morning, "Huh! The main purpose for coming to this city is my career. But, I have been wasting my time by roaming around Malls with Jatin. Even, I ignored calls from my parents. My parents might be thinking that I liked Jatin and I forget about them. Ah! Neel. He might have called me, my phone got switched off," I said to myself and dialed Neel.

"Neel, I am extremely sorry. My phone got switched off" I apologized to Neel. "It's Okay Amisha, I know that you are facing a few struggles with Jatin and found no time to talk to me," said Neel.

"Hmm…I will come to the metro station by 10 O'clock. Will you come there?" I asked Neel.

"Yeah! Definitely. Any time for you," he said and ended the call.

"Neel thinks that I am facing problems here. But, he doesn't know about my comfort zone. Let me not say this truth to Neel, so that he will show some pity on me and help me for my success," I said to myself, got ready, and went to the metro station. We reached WYR Co. Ltd.

together and after the completion of the session, he dropped me outside the hotel and went to his hotel.

The same procedure of going to the company with Neel in the mornings and shopping with Jatin in the evenings continued for fifteen days.

As I am a girl who adapts easily, I completely got accustomed to the City Lifestyle.

The day is the sixteenth day in the city. "Hello Amisha," Neel wished me in the metro station. "Hmm...Come fast. We need to catch the earliest metro. It's high time to attend the important modelling session in company today", I hurriedly boarded the metro.

"Amisha, Be cool. Don't feel tense. Everything will be alright," Neel tried to comfort me.

"Cool? Do you know the importance of today's session? Please don't give any free pieces of advice," I replied to him harshly.

"Okay, Cool! By the way, the dress you wore is not the one that we brought in the mall, right?" Neel questioned me and mistakenly poured some water on my dress while drinking.

"Bah! Do you know the cost of this dress? This is the first gift by Jatin. And, is there any condition to wear only the dress given by you? Shh! Please be quiet for some time," I shouted at him.

Due to some technical issues, the Metro train has stopped before reaching the destination.

"Damn! What happened to this Stupid train? Everything is obstructing me today," I irritated myself.

"Amisha, it seems that the train stops for around twenty minutes. Do you want anything?" Neel asked me?

"Yeah! I need some peace of mind. Will you give that to me?" I ridiculously replied Neel.

After some time, the train started and we both headed towards the company.

After completion of the session, "Hey Neel, are you bored of waiting for me?" I asked Neel. "Let's go," Neel said.

On the metro train, "Thank you so much Neel for always being there for me. You are my best friend. And you are the...," Neel interrupted me.

"Amisha, Is there any work with me?," Neel asked me as I was talking to him in a friendly manner.

"Uh-uh-Actually Yes! I need ten snaps of mine in different stills. How is it possible?" I asked Neel.

Neel quietly gave a small bag to me and said, "Pick your favorite ones"

I was shocked by seeing many of my pictures in distinct poses and dresses. "Golly! How is it possible? Do you know magic?" I thanked Neel.

"When you are trying on different clothes, and posing in front of the mirror outside the trial room, I clicked these pictures in the mall," said Neel.

"Whoa! Thank you so much, Neel. You and your activities are useful for me in one or another way," I said to Neel.

"Thank you for proving me as a useful item," Neel mocked me.

"Item? I didn't say it that way, Neel. Please don't mock me. Are you gone mad? Okay, Let's end this matter here. Jatin might be in his room. He will knock at my room door at 4 p.m. So, we have to rush. I can go to the hotel myself. You may leave if you want," I said to Neel.

With a broken heart, Neel accompanied me quietly to the hotel and went to his hotel in a taxi.

"Attitude is the correct word for Neel. How dare you mock me. Probably I am the only beautiful girl, who is talking to him in a friendly manner. What further can he expect from a future model like me?" I criticized Neel by talking to myself.

"I think that Amisha hardly needs my assistance. She needs only my help, not me. As she got accustomed to everything, she is slowly trying to escape from my positive clutches. I can notice the partial change in Amisha. Amisha is the correct illustration for showing the difference between a village girl and an attitudinal city girl. I never expected this drastic negative change in Amisha. But, what's done is done. As I loved her to my heart, I will not move away from her until she asks me to leave," Neel said to himself.

The next fifteen days passed very moodily for Neel. Neel sees himself as my bodyguard, who accompanies me to the company and drops me in the hotel safely. And the crux of my words shows my disinterest towards Neel. From my attitude, Neel understood that I want any person who nods to my words or a rich person, to whom I will nod my head. As the company asks the girls to showcase themselves in different types of trendy wear, it is uneasy for me to travel in public places like metro rail. I am expecting a car from Neel's side. But Neel is not a rich person to maintain his car. I kept on expecting something from Neel without thinking of reverting him for his help.

On the other hand, except for the matter of Neel, everything is fine for me. Neel has become a burden for me. For the past fifteen days, no day has passed without showing my anger towards Neel. By looking at my friends who come in a car to the company, Neel became very cheap for me.

CHAPTER SEVENTEEN

My heart for 'him' and Break up with 'him'

I rushed to the company quickly as the new trainer will take charge from Miss Fara today. But, by the time I reached the hall, the lecture had started. My co-students have formed around by joining their hands and from the gaps of the round, I could see a man from the backside with a Fitted suit, Derby shoes, and a luxury watch. I went to them and as the official was facing the other side of the group, I said, "Excuse me, sir." When he turned his head, I was shocked by seeing him.

"Huh! Jat...," the official interrupted me.

"Hello! Can I know your name?" the official asked.

"Eh! I am uh-uh- Amisha," I replied.

"Hello Ms. Amisha, Welcome to the second stage of your training," he said.

"I will be back with your trainer," the official informed everyone and went away.

"What the hell is happening around me? How come Jatin in this company? Is he working here itself or err-Ah-I am confused. Why is he behaving casually even after seeing me? What's the ploy? Ugh! His casualness is scaring me more. This will be the last day of my career. This is the biggest lie I have ever said to my parents. I can't envisage the predictions after this fuss. Huh! I have to live in a village as a failure. I ponder that my parents will not even allow me to come out from now," Jatin interrupted my thoughts.

"Hello Beautiful Ladies, I am Jatin, MD of the WYR Co. Ltd. Meet Miss Alia who took charge from Miss Fara. Miss Alia stood as the winner in two contests conducted by our company and stood as the runner-up in one contest. She will train you for the rest of this month" said Jatin. Throughout the session, my eyes focussed completely on Jatin. But Jatin is giving a random look at me.

After the completion of the session, I came out and along with Neel, I went to the metro station. I didn't inform Neel anything about the incident in the company as we have been maintaining the silence for the past fifteen days. And my ego stopped me from breaking the silence.

I went into the hotel and noticed that my hotel room was open. Guessing Jatin's presence in the room, I stepped in by saying, "Excuse me?"

"No, I am not going to excuse you. How dare you cheat not only me but my whole family. Acting will be a perfect career option for you rather than Modelling. Shucks! You are a great actor. I don't want to waste my time with bloody talks. Go and pack your luggage, I will throw you in front of your parents. Pshaw! Be in your village and engage in the household activity. That suits you. Some Jobless stranger comes for you, marries, and takes you to another remote area. Don't you consider yourself as a lucky girl for having a gentleman like me? At least you might have confessed the truth to me. You made a very big blunder Amisha. Even if I excuse you, your parents are not going to spare you. You have to face consequences for all this drama," Jatin shouted at me.

"Jatin, I am extremely sorry. My intention is not to disturb you. I love modelling. I cheated all of you only for this profession," I howled and sat on my knees by bending my head in front of Jatin.

"Hee-hee!," Listening to the laughter, I raised my head and saw Jatin laughing.

"Jatin, why are you laughing? Is this the time to laugh? I didn't crack any jokes," I asked Jatin.

"Ha-ha, You are expecting these criticisms from me, right? For your satisfaction, I rebuked you," said Jatin.

"I didn't get you, Jatin. What are you trying to say exactly?," I asked Jatin.

"I created this big fuss just to scare you. As I am from the modelling profession, I always dreamt of marrying a girl from this field. But my parents pressured me to marry a girl from the village because they believed that the girls from the village background knew the proper culture. Yes! I liked you when the marriage mediator showed your picture, but I somewhere felt that I am not completely happy and satisfied. This is the reason for pressurizing you in your village to wear a trendy dress," said Jatin.

I listened to Jatin's words and said, "Is this real?"

"Ha-ha. Yes, this is true," said Jatin.

I unbelievably believed him and said, "Thank you Jatin."

"No more formalities between us from now. Now, you are a complete fiancée to me," said Jatin.

I just smiled at him. The day ended unexpectedly and peacefully.

The next day, "Amisha, Are you ready? Let's go," said Jatin.

"Please wait in the parking lot for me. I will be there in five minutes," I said.

When I stepped out of the lift, I saw Neel at the reception who was staring at me. I went to him and said, "Jatin will take care of me from now. If you think of me as a burden, you are permitted to return to your village."

"Your village? Does that village belong only to me? Also, I never felt you as a burden. But as I am a useless person for you, I will go far from you. I can recognize the drastic change in you... I mean in the Negative sense. You are not the Amisha whom I met in the village. You are in the clutches of this very dangerous city lifestyle. Take care of yourself. Goodbye," Neel told me.

"Ack! I am not free to listen to all this Blah-blah. Jatin might be waiting for me in the car. I am in a hurry. Can you clear me the way to go?," I showed my attitude and went away."

CHAPTER EIGHTEEN

My feet got wet to walk on the Ramp

In the Company, "Mam, could you please follow me?" asked the receptionist.

I followed her and she asked me to wait before the CEO's cabin. After a few minutes, she called me to enter the cabin.

"Good morning sir," I greeted the CEO.

"A very good morning Ami," the CEO replied.

"Sir, my name is Amisha, not Ami," I said to the CEO.

"Yeah! I know. But Ami is the most suitable name for you. Like your presence, character, and behavior, you have to change your name too. Anyway, the reason for calling you is 'you'," he said.

"Sir?," I questioned.

"Hee-hee, I mean that your grace and style made you sit before me. You got selected to represent our company in the Miss south zone competition," the CEO said.

"Miss South zone? Whoa! I can't believe this. Thank you so much sir," I thanked the CEO.

"Hope you succeed in the competition and bring good fame to our company. All the best," the CEO wished me.

I shared this news with Jatin who also felt happy and wished me good luck.

"I know that I am the best among all my co-models in this company. I anticipated this. The CEO took the correct decision by selecting me for the competition. I am the only person eligible to bring the crown for WYR Co. Ltd," I expressed my overconfidence to Jatin.

"Hey! Jatin, can you convince my parents by saying that the shopping has not yet been completed and we need one more month. There are only fifteen days left for the competition," I asked Jatin.

"Yeah! I will do that for you. But, please don't be overconfident, Amisha. That will leave you in trouble," Jatin said to me.

"Call me Ami," I said to Jatin.

After ten days, In a shopping mall, "What would you like to shop, Ami?," Jatin asked me.

"The trendy wear," I replied.

I shopped for different types of tops, skirts, trousers, and frocks for the competition. The bill in the billing counter showed sixty thousand rupees.

"Oh! It's just sixty thousand rupees. How cheap? City life is easily affordable nowadays. Can you pay the bill? I will be waiting in the car" I said to Jatin and went to the parking lot.

"Sir, who is that madam?," the shop owner asked Jatin.

"She is a model under training," Jatin replied.

"Oh! Will she do an advertisement for our mall?" the shop owner asked.

"How would I know? You might have asked her," Jatin replied.

"Sir, as you are madam's secretary, I am asking you," the shop owner replied.

Jatin, with a rude face, rushed out after paying the bill.

When Jatin told me the entire incident, I was enraged by saying, "Advertisement for a mall? How am I looking? How can he expect a beautiful and a future model like me to shoot for a mall's advertisement?" Jatin comforted me and we both reached the hotel after having dinner.

The day of the Miss south zone competition arrived. I and Jatin entered the set where everyone was busy setting up lights, posters, and chairs. By looking at the entire set, I got tense. We walked in search of our allotted room backstage. I could see the alluring and prepossessing contestants. They reflected their voguishness and stylishness. When we are walking to our room, I sensed the Negative vibes. The atmosphere surrounding me is pressurizing me and it completely tensed me. My contestant number is 16.

The competition has started with the traditional look. All contestants wore the cultural dress of their respective villages for this round. But I wore a Ghagra Choli as I always consider the cultural dress of my village as cheap. The dress which is similar to my village cultural wear is worn by one of the judges who received many praising words for her look. I felt sad for not wearing it.

My turn has come. I stepped on the ramp and managed to walk in high heels. While walking, I could figure out that my walk is not perfect when compared to the walk of other contestants.

I came backstage and found no one to share my feelings with. As Jatin is the MD of WYR Co. Ltd., he is busy making arrangements and conversing with other officials.

The next round is the Western round for which the clothes were given by the organizers themselves as it would help in promoting different brands. I felt very happy to get a Bodycon dress, which is my favorite trendy wear.

I confidently let my hair down and with a broad smile, I stepped on the ramp. But, the focus of the lights disturbed me. The focus of the lights for this round was increased, which distracted me. Somehow, I walked and came down.

I felt very sad and stood waiting for the Qualifiers list. The host put the mic near her mouth announcing the results, "The contestants who got qualified for the next round are Contestant numbers 3,7,11,13,18,21....."

"Huh! My number? These judges are not qualified to judge this competition, they couldn't find the grace in me. They lost an opportunity to announce me as the winner. But just in the south zone of the state, there is tough competition. How can I represent myself in the National level competition?" I said to myself and went to Jatin with discontentment.

CHAPTER NINETEEN

I CALLED MY BLUFF

"Hurry up! Quick! Go and sit in the car. I will follow you," Jatin said to me hurriedly.

"What happened, Jatin? Is anything wrong?" I asked Jatin.

"Yes, everything has gone wrong. I am feeling ashamed to face the officials of other companies. Our company's fame has gone in vain. Can't you notice that? We have to rush from here before listening to many criticisms," said Jatin.

In the car, "Jatin, how did the CEO feel?" I asked Jatin.

"He is feeling very bad. He dialed me and regretted saying that he had made the wrong decision for the first time. Do you know? From the past ten years, the representatives of our company never failed in the first level itself. Everyone tried to push themselves up to the Semi-finals. Also, two girls stood as the winners of this Miss South Zone competition," said Jatin.

"I have done no wrong. I tried to give my best, the focus lights troubled me," I said.

"Oh! There is no wrong from your side. Isn't it?," asked Jatin. "Yeah!," I replied.

"Then, how did all the girls manage to do extraordinarily well? You are the only one who utterly got flopped in managing with costumes, makeup, expressions, Body language, and everything," said Jatin.

"It's just a competition. No need to take it more seriously," I said.

"You are stretching your life by just presuming yourself like the queen and seeing you in the sky. You are completely in the world of desire, come out of it and face the actual world. You are considering this south zone competition as "Just a competition" but it's a life decider. You know Merina right?," asked Jatin.

"Yes, she is the closest friend of Miss Evana and also one of the finest models," I replied

"Yeah! She started her career by winning this 'just' competition. You know about her huge fame now. She got many opportunities after this competition. She didn't say 'no' even for small photoshoots. She handled every opportunity with due care and didn't consider any competition as 'just a competition," said Jatin.

"You are talking too much Jatin. Miss Evana, the top model, started her career by giving her first audition to the National Level Competition. She got selected in auditions, reached Semi-finals, and stood as the winner of the prestigious competition. What would you answer for this?," I asked Jatin.

"It seems that you always consider only Miss Evana as the model right? Alright, I can answer you. Do you know Miss Vanya?," asked Jatin.

"Yes. She is one of the oldest models who brought up this modeling career to heights," I said.

"Miss Evana is the daughter of Miss Vanya. I think you got the answer," said Jatin.

"Oh! what do you mean?" I asked.

"As Miss Vanya was the model, she always wanted to see her daughter as a model. So, she strived to make Evana a model. And from the age of eight years only, Evana got trained for being a great model. She struggled a lot to get this huge success. From that tender age itself, she used to wear fashionable clothes, and do you know, there is a ramp in their home itself for practicing the walk," said Jatin.

"Really? I don't know about this struggling past behind her success," I said.

"Every success story will have a difficult past behind it. You will be successful only after struggling yourself," Jatin said.

These words of Jatin made me think about my overconfidence.

After fifteen days, "I completed my training program from the WYR Co. Ltd. What else now?" I asked Jatin.

"You got few opportunities for photoshoots right?," said Jatin.

"Yeah! But I am not interested in doing them," I replied.

"You have to try all the chances you get, then only you will be a successful person," Jatin said.

"Is there any obligation for a model to try all the professions?" I questioned.

First of all, please don't consider yourself a model. Who declared you as a model? You just got trained. Remember this. Okay, even after listening to the stories of Miss Merina and Miss Evana, you haven't changed yourself," said Jatin.

"Okay, I will approve all the opportunities and prove to you that there will be no use in working with these low fame companies," I challenged Jatin.

"No need to approve the opportunities for my sake. You should have immense interest in that field before accepting the proposals," Jatin said, criticizing me.

CHAPTER TWENTY

THE PARTIAL REALIZATION

After two days, I received a message for a Saree Photoshoot. I went to the given place and was shocked by seeing hundreds of people there.

"Hey! step inside," a person called me.

"I entered inside and stood aside. They threw a saree at me and said, "Wear this."

"Please try to talk with respect," I said to them.

"Respect? The models waiting outside will work with no respect. If you want respect, you can leave," they shouted at me.

I controlled myself and asked, "where is the room to wear a saree?"

"Room? Can you see? This room is complete with ladies. Wear it here itself," they said.

With no other option, I wore the saree, went to the shooting room, and stood before the camera.

"Give a pose", the cameraman asked me.

I kept both of my hands on my waist and slightly turned my entire body

"Mam, are you a model?" the cameraman asked.

"Yeah! How do you know?" I questioned him.

"I can sense it from the pose you gave. Are you a failure in Modelling?" the cameraman asked.

"Nope! I just didn't win in one competition," I said.

"That's a failure," the cameraman criticized me.

The word 'Failure' from the words of the cameraman made me think about myself. I questioned myself, "Am I a failure?"

After a few days, I went to another photoshoot.

No one gave me due respect there. They gave me a dress and asked me to wait until my turn came. I waited for an hour. My patience has decreased. So, I directly went to the coordinator and complained about the delay.

"How long are you here for?" the coordinator asked me.

"Sir, I have been sitting like an idol for an hour," I answered.

"An hour? Do you mean one hour? How silly? Once, look at the ladies standing there. They were continuously standing from this morning. Now it's noon. What will you say to them? It's called Patience. Feel happy to have a chair to sit on," the coordinator said, pointing his fingers towards the two ladies who stood very uncomfortably. Seeing myself in a better position, I went and waited for my turn.

After a few days, I contested for a small modelling competition in my district. There I could see a few ladies facing many humiliations. Also, few women entered this career with no support.

From all these series of incidents, I learnt many things. I faced criticism, saw people who were struggling in this career with no support by waiting outside the companies, and shooting offices for a chance. I also came across models who are facing many humiliations from men. The key thing I learnt is 'Patience.' I realized that one's fury is not the solution, but one's patience will lay the path to the solution.

CHAPTER TWENTY-ONE

THE SECOND OPPORTUNITY AND THE FIRST SUCCESS

Once, Jatin came to me by shouting, "Amisha...Amisha... Where are you."

"What happened?," I asked Jatin.

"I brought good news for you," Jatin replied.

"Hmm, is it about a boring photo shoot?" I asked disappointedly.

"Nope! Guess what?" he asked.

"I don't have time to guess. Please say it," I said.

"Oh! You have become a busy person. You don't even have time to guess," Jatin mocked me.

"Huh! Please don't lag this issue. I want to attend a shoot. I am in a hurry to get ready for it" I said.

"Oh! I think I have disturbed you. Please proceed," Jatin said with upset.

"What's the news?" I asked.

"No. Nothing," Jatin replied as a counter to me.

"Okay, I will come for dinner with you tonight. Is this okay?" I asked Jatin.

"Yes! I will reveal the news now," Jatin said excitedly by giving a letter.

I got elated by reading that. A well-known company in which my favorite model Miss Evana trained wrote to me by offering an audition to the 'Melina Style icon' competition that happens every two years.

I immediately accepted the proposal and prepared to represent myself as a rich and confident girl in the contest. I and Jatin went shopping for a few clothes for the competition. Jatin sat aside and I shopped around twelve types of different clothes.

After ten days, Jatin once entered my room and asked, "Will our marriage happen?.'

"What happened? Why are you asking about it suddenly?" I asked.

"Your mother made me pose this question to you. Your mom called me and said that enough shopping is done for the engagement. She reiterated that there is only one month left for the engagement and asked us to come to the village," said Jatin.

"Oh! What shall we do now?" I asked.

"I have no clue. I think it's better to facc your mother and let her know all the matter," Jatin said.

"Ummm! But what if she won't send me back to the city. I don't want to miss this golden opportunity. Jatin, please try to manage my mom for a month. Only you can do it." I pleaded with Jatin. Jatin somehow convinced my mom.

After five days, we both went to the Audition spot. I didn't feel tense even by seeing many models from different places. I observed their personality, dressing style, make-up, walking style, and body fitness and tried to incorporate the positive things in me. I am just confident, but not overconfident about the auditions. I became an optimistic, patient, and adjustable person mainly because of the small photoshoots. I attended this competition after my first failure. But, even now, the behavior of considering me as a queen and others as people of low status continued in me.

I dressed up in a white bustier top with a denim pencil skirt, went onto the ramp confidently by letting my hair down, and walked elegantly. From the ramp itself, I could figure out that the audience was giving an awful look at my style.

After coming backstage, many models are whispering about my casualness on the ramp. Even one model came to me and said, "When you entered this set, everyone including me gave a weird look at you as you came by just wearing a casual dress with a messy ponytail. Everyone considered you not a competition. But you surprised all of us with your style. Some magic in you can admire anyone. Keep it up." I took the model's words for granted as I already anticipated these praises.

In the next round, the models have to present themselves traditionally. I didn't wander outside unnecessarily like others because if I turn up on the stage directly, the audience will see me with sparkling looks. Everyone wore a saree with many ornaments and walked in their respective styles.

As expected, the audience cheered me while I was walking in a Short Patli style saree draping by adding a retro essence to it. Very rarely, people see models in different styles during the traditional round, so all people encouraged me for my different looks and efforts.

After some time, the host announced the selected candidates for the mega competition. Overall, thirty-five candidates got selected including me from the auditions.

After the Auditions, I went to the hotel and informed Jatin about the entire contest. He appreciated me and said, "Do you know? Miss Evana is going to be the Judge for the final round of the contest."

"Whoa! I can't believe it. Is it real?" I was surprised.

"And also the winner gets a chance to have dinner with her. Hope you have a prospect," Jatin said.

"I will strive for that moment. I won't let that opportunity go in vain. I am confident that I will be the one who dines with Miss Evana," I said.

After fifteen days, on the day of the competition, "Are you ready to face the ramp?," asked Jatin.

"Yes, I am. I will get onto the ramp as a rich and confident girl," I said.

"Hope you succeed in the first level. All the best," Jatin said.

"Don't worry, I will be the one who carries the crown," I said.

One of the coordinators of the contest came to me, handed over a dress, and said, "This is the brand you need to wear and promote."

"I can look after my hair and face," I said to the make-up man and the hairstylist. I didn't listen to their words. They even tried to convince me by saying that my look will be unique if they take care of me.

I got ready, came out of my room, and went backstage as the first level was about to start.

After a few minutes, I entered the ramp wearing a pink-colored maxi dress with a pearl jewellery set. I walked like a rich and elegant girl with a broad smile.

After the first level completion, I stood backstage with the huge confidence of qualifying for the next round.

In the contest, all the models are supposed to be backstage and there will be a person who calls the qualifiers onto the stage because we can't hear the voice of a person on the stage from backstage. I am waiting for my turn to go onto the stage.

Then, the host announced, "I consider it as a great honor to welcome Mr. Bhardwaj, the manager of the Outlook clothing brand onto the stage for announcing the names of qualifiers."

I am curiously waiting for my contestant number. After a few seconds, I realized that I was in shock as my number was not announced. I was completely disappointed with the results and went into my room hastily. I shut the door and sat alone by considering myself as an unfortunate girl. My heart got filled with huge sadness. I am completely disconsolate about this happening. The tears are not even rolling down from my eyes as it is a sudden blow that put me in this situation. I tried to find the reason for my disqualification.

CHAPTER TWENTY-TWO

FORTUITOUS MEETING WITH HIM ENLIGHTENED ME

After thinking about an hour, I shouted, "I want the reason for disqualifying me."

My room door opened slowly and I heard, "I will answer you."

I instantly turned my face and got shocked by seeing him. "Neel? How come you are in this rich contest," I asked Neel.

"The answer for your failure is in you," he said.

"Me? I performed well, in fact, I am the only model who showcased myself richly. Firstly, stop judging me." I said.

"Rich...Rich...Rich...Does modeling mean richness? You got locked in the hands of this city and luxurious life. Even the money you are spending is not earned by you. Then, how do you know the value of a rupee? You are not trying to ramp on the stage as a 'model', but you are desiring yourself as a 'rich girl' on the ramp. Showcasing yourself as a rich girl will not make you the best model. This unnecessary stuff will let you down. If you still consider yourself as a rich person, you can't accept the crown even in the smallest contest, because the people who are fond of being rich will always see things as inferior, they can't adjust to the situation. The wrong is in you Amisha. Correct it," Neel said.

"First of all, why are you here?" I asked Neel.

Then, Jatin entered my room and said, "Mr. Bharadwaj, please take a seat. How can I digest myself if you stand? It's a huge surprise to see you here. Can I know the reason for your presence here?"

"Bharadwaj? He is Neel right? How do you know him?" I questioned Jatin about Neel.

"Hey, who doesn't know about this celebrity," Jatin said.

"Celebrity? Are you kidding?" I said.

"No, I am not. He is Mr. Neel Bharadwaj, manager of the Outlook clothing brand. He is the one who announced the qualifiers list," said Jatin.

"Mr. Neel Bharadwaj? Did you take revenge on me by not reading my name from the list?" I asked Neel.

"Firstly, thank you so much, Amisha. It is because of you I am in this respectable position. Because of your heart-breaking words, I got depressed and decided to teach a lesson to you. Before handling a 'Rich' girl like you, I want to be in an eminent position right? So, you are the sole reason for my success. In between, I didn't take revenge. I taught you a lesson," said Neel.

"But, but how did you become the manager of such a leading company?" Amisha asked.

"Do you know my educational qualifications? I have done my post-graduation in Fashion Modeling. I am the first person in our city to go abroad for studies. I also worked with many eminent models abroad. Finding a career in our country is just a piece of cake for me. I liked you and I especially loved your determination and interest in Modelling. So, I thought of encouraging you for your success. I didn't tell you about my profession because, as a loving boy, I expected the same love from your side for me, not for my profession. If I had revealed my identity earlier, you might have taken that as a chance and moved affectionately with me for your selfishness right? Now your misconduct has been revealed," Neel said.

"Huh! You are a big liar," I said.

"You are the big cheater. How can you label me as a liar? I have done many things for you. I have sacrificed some of my important days for you. Before all, I loved you. Ugh! but you fooled me. Leave about showing affection and love towards me, you at least didn't consider me as a person," Neel shouted.

"But..." (Neel interrupted me)

"Once rewind your life in the village and compare it with the present one. I saw no girl in my life like you. You are like a chameleon, you change your behavior as per your comfort. You won't be concerned about others. Two months ago, you were the girl who gave a weird look towards the people wearing a shirt and jeans and now you are the 'Rich' girl who is looking awkwardly towards the people wearing churidar. How can you change immensely within two months? You are the girl who dreamt of being a model, but now you are the girl desiring to be a rich girl. Can you notice the huge difference and change?" Neel said.

"Neel...I'm..." (Neel interrupted me)

"Stop there. I don't want to listen to you anymore. Think with your heart. You will find the right answer," said Neel and went away.

Jatin stood in one of the corners of the room, listened to the whole conversation, and understood about my past.

"I don't want to stress you by asking about the relationship between both of you. Take your time," said Jatin and left the place.

I was reminded about my changes, faults, behavior, and everything that I have done for Neel. I felt really bad and questioned myself, "Am I that stupid? Don't I have common sense? How painful will it be?"

After a while, I vacated the room, went to Jatin, and said "I am sorry if I have troubled you."

Jatin said, "Not at all. Come, let's go out and dine"

"No, the expenses in the restaurants are too much. Let's go to our hotel," I said.

"Hey, no need to bury our small desires for success, people around you just expect some love and affection from you. That's it," said Jatin.

CHAPTER TWENTY-THREE

MY PARENTS AND MY PASSION

After two days, "Jatin, I got an offer from a leading company to represent them in the Fashion week that was going to be conducted by 'Marris Products,' I said to Jatin.

"Wow! Such a wonderful chance. Hope you utilize this in a better way and top the contest. This time, I am completely confident about you," said Jatin.

"Jatin, I want my parents to be here on the day of the contest," I said to Jatin.

"Why? Don't you know the consequences? What is the need for their presence now? How will you go for the contest if they come here?" Jatin questioned me.

"I don't want their mere presence, I want them to see me on the ramp," I said.

"Are you gone mad? Once you think about your goal, your career will be at stake if we call them," said Jatin.

"Jatin, in these times, I need huge encouragement and a bit of fear. I can get these with the presence of my parents. My parents' presence among the audience is an encouragement for me and I will be within my limits with a little bit of fear. At least in their presence, to keep up their name, I will strive to win this time," I said.

"Your words are making sense. But we need to be very careful, otherwise, your mom will take you away from here even before going to the contest," Jatin said.

I dialed my parents and asked them to come to the city to witness a few sightseeing places in this beautiful rainy season. My parents agreed to it.

After a few days, They came to the city. Jatin went to the Railway station to pick them up.

"How are you? my dear son-in-law," asked my mother.

"I am good. Hope the journey went well," Jatin said.

"Not that good. Why did you book our tickets in the AC compartment? I and your father-in-law shivered the entire night," my mom said.

"Oh! from now on, I will book tickets after asking your opinion. Come, let's go to the hotel," Jatin said.

"God! Such a big one. What is the need of living in this huge hotel? It's a complete waste of money. Why don't you take a small room?," my mom asked Jatin.

Jatin remembered the 'free' trick told by me and said, "the rent will be paid by the company. It's completely free."

"If it's free, then there is no problem," said my mom.

"Mom! Dad! How are you? It's been more than two months since I saw you," I said.

"I am feeling glad to see you in Churidaar. I saw many women wearing shirts and jeans that got torn here and there. Don't they feel ashamed for wearing those kinds of filthy clothes? The mistake is with their parents. How can they...," I interrupted my mom.

"Let it be mom, it's their culture," I said.

"Culture? How can you term this as a culture? People here are following a very bad system here," my mom said.

My mom controlled her anger towards the modern culture and asked, "Jatin, you have booked four return tickets to the village right?"

"Why mom? Uh-err-What's the problem?" I asked my mom tensely.

"Why is it sweating Amisha? Why are you feeling tense?" my mom asked.

"Hmm-err-nothing mom. I am just-err-anyway what is the need of coming to the village?" I asked my mom.

"There are only a few days left for your engagement. Once, I already postponed the engagement date for you people. Don't you remember that? I sent you to the city for shopping purposes only. Your work got completed right?" my mom asked. With no other clue, I said yes to my mom.

CHAPTER TWENTY-FOUR

FULFILLING MY DREAM BY DIVULGING MYSELF TO MY PARENTS

On the day of the competition, in the morning, "Jatin...Jatin...Where is Amisha? I couldn't find her anywhere in the hotel. Where did she go?," my mom asked Jatin.

"Don't be tense, mother-in-law. Your daughter improved herself in cooking food. She became a master chef. As there is one cooking competition in our city today, she went there," Jatin managed.

"I am happy about it. But, why didn't she inform us earlier?" my mom asked.

"Hmm, it's a surprise for you. Come let's go there and encourage her," Jatin said.

"Yeah! Definitely. She must be the winner," my mom blessed me indirectly and came to the spot with my father.

"Please take a seat, I will be back," Jatin said.

"Jatin, why are the posters looking different? Banners should be related to the cooking competition right?" asked my mom.

"Well...Um, er, I will find out the reason and let you know," Jatin said and came to my room backstage.

"Amisha, your mom is asking many doubts. I can't manage her. What shall we do now?" Jatin asked me.

"Don't face her. Try to skip from her eyes," I said.

"What?," Jatin questioned me.

"Yes! She won't leave this place as she doesn't know the route to return to the hotel. My parents have no choice except to sit among the audience," I said.

"Good idea! Be strong and don't feel tense," Jatin said.

The contest has started. The first round is a traditional round for which each model is stepping onto the ramp with their respective styles.

"What's going on? Is this a Modelling competition? Why am I here? Where did the Jatin and Amisha go?" my mother yelled with confusion.

In this round, I walked on the ramp wearing a pant-style black saree with a high ponytail and white stone jewellery set.

"Mad! Why did this girl wear a dupatta on her trousers? Do they have common sense? Look at her hair. She got her hair painted with all the rainbow colors. Ack! These women...," my father interrupted my mom.

"It's our Amisha, put on your specs and look at her," my father said.

"Amisha? Yes, she is our girl. Huh! I can't believe this. How come she is here?" my mom said.

"I think she is another girl who resembles our baby. I am correct right?" my dad said.

"Ufff! Yeah, there is a chance. But, where are they both?" my mom asked.

"I think we have missed the exact address of the cooking competition. So, Jatin might have gone in search of the exact location. Don't feel tense, after finding the correct spot, Jatin will take us from here," my dad said.

The second round has started which is an introductory round in a western look.

I entered the ramp wearing a glitzy Mermaid Silhouette dress.

"Amisha? I am sure. It's our girl. But I can't believe it. I am not going to bear it anymore. How can she cheat us?" my mom was enraged.

I took the mic and said "Hello Everyone! I am Amisha, an eighteen-year-old girl. Determination is the word that suits me a lot. Follow your dreams is the quote that I follow in my life. I want to show the world that I am a confident girl with a big heart. I am the girl who always dreamt about my passion. When I was in my mother's womb, she dreamt about her child full of confidence and compassion. Now, I have grown up with double confidence and following my passion. A girl feels confident when she steps into the field of her interest. As modelling is my interest, I am confident to speak now. How can one expect a girl to be confident in the sphere which she doesn't like? My mother's dream gets fulfilled only when I go with my passion. I am here to fulfill her dream. No matter if she likes my passion or not. She is mine and I have to make her happy. The biggest thing I achieved till now is the presence of my parents' in this competition. With their presence, I am considering myself as the queen."

After a while, by listening to the audience's cheerful sounds for my speech, my mom's anger got reduced. My speech has touched her heart. Tears from my mom's eyes were rolling down with mixed feelings of joy, satisfaction, contentment, and fulfillment. Claps by people changed my mom's mindset towards this field. My mom with happiness saw my father and said, "Look at your daughter. She is our pride." My father, wiping his tears, replied by saying, "Yes! She made us feel proud. From now on, everyone in the village recognizes us like the father and mother of Miss Amisha."

The results were announced and I stood as one among the five finalists of the Contest.

Jatin noticed my parents' happiness, went to them, and said, "See your daughter Amisha. She is a model and she stood as an inspiration to many others. Did you listen to her speech? Be proud of being parents for a daughter like Amisha. She didn't come to this position easily. She faced many struggles to reach this stage. She is a hard worker. Won't you appreciate her?"

"Yes, I want to meet her immediately. She defeated us and reached the highest stage in our hearts. She proved herself. Where is she?" asked my mom.

Jatin and my parents came backstage and knocked at my room door. As I don't know about the positive change from my parents, I expected a slap on my cheek from my mom. But, she came in and by looking into my eyes, she said, "You won. You proved all of my assumptions as wrong. I am sorry for...," I interrupted my mom.

"Don't apologize, mom. I am your daughter forever. You have the sole right to judge, question, or control me. Because of you, I am here. As a mother from an orthodox family, you correctly tried to protect me. But as I am committed to my passion, I cheated you. I am extremely sorry for cheating you both. I did this for the welfare of our family. Hope you understand," I said to my mom, giving her a happy hug.

"Be happy, my daughter," my father expressed his ultimate happiness in one word.

They both blessed and wished me for the final round.

Keeping in mind the words of my parents, I entered the ramp by wearing a white-colored fish cut frock with an Emerald set of jewellery. I walked more fashionably, more stylishly, and more attractively with more confidence.

"And the three finalists of the Marris Products Miss Fashion week contest are...are...one among them is Emma," the host announced.

My heartbeat suddenly started beating fast. I am covering my shivering hands with my dress. I am frequently brushing my hair with my hands to cover my eyes that have turned red with tension.

After a few seconds, the host put the mic near his mouth, waited for a few more seconds, and said, "And the last two finalists are Lia and Amisha."

I took a deep breath and saw the happiest faces of my parents.

And for the last round, the host asked me to choose a chit from a bowl. I took one and gave it to him. He opened it and said, "The question for you should be asked by one of the judges who is currently not present here. She will reach here within ten minutes. In the meantime, let's complete the questioning round for remaining models."

"What the hell is happening here? Why did this happen only for my daughter? God, please don't make her feel tense. Hope that the judge comes fast," my mother said to herself.

After fifteen minutes, suddenly, the escorts surrounding the set turned back and walked towards a white car. Everyone turned their heads with anxiety and they immediately stood from their respective seats. Even the judges stood from the couch and held bouquets in their hands. I am unable to see the person who came out of the car as everyone is surrounding her. "Why is this special welcome for this person? Why are they creating a scene here?" I said to myself.

After a few minutes, I saw her foot with red-colored high heels and black-colored nail polish. As the crowd got reduced, I saw her slender hands which were as soft as cotton.

The bodyguards around her cleared the crowd and it is..it's Miss Evana. I never imagined meeting such a top model in my life, but the day has come for me. I controlled my excitement and stood formally.

After a few minutes, she got seated and the host said, "Miss Evana, a grand welcome for you. Please pose a question to the finalist Amisha."

"Hello Amisha, the question is, 'when will you feel happy?' This question may look like a crazy one. But your answer shows your control and respect towards your emotions," Miss Evana said.

"Hello Miss Evana, I felt happy when my parents felt very proud of me and said, 'You have won'. Winning the hearts of one's parents is more than enough for any person in the world. This position, this opportunity, this field, this audience, these claps are not equal to the honest praising words of my parents. The sole reason for my smiling face is my parents who sat among the audience. Their presence gave me this confidence to speak boldly and confidently," I replied.

Immediately, the whole set quaked with the clapping sounds.

The host welcomed Miss Evana onto the stage by saying, "It's time to announce the results. May I call Miss Evana, the Miss Fashion week 2019 for crowning the Miss Fashion week 2020"

"Miss Fashion week 2019? Is Miss Evana the Miss Fashion week in the last year? I don't know about this?" I said to myself.

Miss Evana came onto the stage, took a card from the host, and announced, "The second runner up of this Marris Products Miss Fashion week 2020 is Miss Emma."

I hold my breath as there is more chance of winning for me now. Everyone in the audience is very keen to know the winner. My mom just closed her eyes and continuously prayed to god. I am reflecting my smile outside and controlling my stress inside.

Miss Evana announced, "And the winner of the Marris Products Miss Fashion week 2020 is...."

"Huh! Please announce it. I can't control my feelings. It's stressful for me," I said to myself.

Miss Evana took the mic closer to her lips and announced "The Miss Fashion week 2020 is...it's none other than MISS AMISHA."

I can't express my happiness. The tears covered my eyes which obstructed me from seeing the happiness of my parents. I stood in one place and shedded my happy tears. I sat on a couch arranged for the winner and Miss Evana stood behind me. She removed the crown on her head and placed it on my head that giving me goosebumps.

My mother in the audience was crying with happiness. I hugged Miss Evana and waved my hand towards the audience.

After a while, I went to my mom and placed the crown on her as my gratitude for her. She shed her tears and hugged me.

The CEO of the WYR Co. Ltd. who came there congratulated me and said "You brought out the hidden Amisha in you. Now, you are the best." I apologized to him for my ill-mannered behaviour and assured him of representing WYR Co. Ltd. in a further contest.

An official came to me and asked me and my parents to follow him. We went to a large hall where a lot of media channels were waiting for my interview. The cameras focussed my parents and prided them. Later, we moved to another hall where Miss Evana was waiting for us.

"Come, Miss Amisha. Have a seat. Congratulations dear, you did extraordinarily well," Miss Evana praised me, congratulated and greeted my parents.

"Thank you so much, ma'am. Listening to the word 'Miss Amisha' from your mouth is adding to my happiness," I said to Miss Evana.

"Call me Miss Evana, no need for any formalities," Miss Evana said.

"No ma'am, I can't. Addressing you with respect is not a formality for me. How can one call their *guru* with the name? I came to this position by seeing you. You are my true inspiration. Thank you for inspiring me ma'am," I said to Miss Evana.

MY DREAM HAS COME TRUE

9 798885 305334